The Book With No Words

By A. P. Veidmark

Illustrated by Mary Beth Benton

The Book With No Words

By A. P. Veidmark
Illustrated by Mary Beth Benton
Layout & Design by Pixel Parfait, LLC

Hill·Clark & Associates

Published in the United States
First Edition

A.P. Veidmark dedicates this book to all the books with no words.

Mary Beth Benton dedicates this book to Andy — for always believing in her.

Once there was a book
with no words.
The book was about a little boy
named Zack.

When this book was published, Zack learned that there were no words in his book. That worried Zack.

What? No words!

"No children will be able to read my book," Zack thought.
"What kind of a book has no words?"

When Zack's book was shelved in the library, he saw all of the children reading books with words.

Zack's book sat on the shelf for days, weeks and even months, until one day a little boy took it off the shelf.

Uh oh!

Zack shook with fear.
This was the first time his book
had been picked up by a child.

Zack was afraid that the boy would not like a book with no words.
Zack thought his book would be tossed aside when the boy saw
that there was nothing to read.

When the boy opened the book he started laughing.

Other kids saw the boy laughing
and came to see what
was so funny.

Soon all the kids were pointing and laughing at Zack's book. Zack was devastated!

Zack thought they were making fun of his book.
After all, what kind of a book has no words?

But Zack was wrong! The children were laughing because his book had funny pictures.

That day Zack found out that
he was in a picture book.
There were not supposed to be words.

Now more and more children were looking at Zack's book. They laughed with delight.

Zack swam with joy!
He loved being the star in a
picture book!

There is one word
hidden in Zack's book.
Can you find it?

About the Author

A.P. Veidmark was born and raised in Glendale, Arizona. He wrote this story when he was in the fifth grade. His teacher suggested that he publish it. As an adult, his hobbies are scuba diving, outdoor sports, camping, mountain biking, cooking outdoors, skydiving, long walks on the beach and traveling (especially road trips with his son).

.

About the Illustrator

Mary Beth Benton's other works include *Bub and the Nut* by Henderson (2004), *Digging for Bones* by Matte (2011), *Special Delivery* by Isley (2013), *Fuz and the Skunk* by Isley (2015). Currently she is working with her husband, on a children's book titled *Hathi*. She is a member of the Society for Children's Book Writers and Illustrators.

Mary Beth was born in Michigan and moved to Arizona at the age of five. She lived on the Navajo/Hopi reservations where her mother was a nurse. The mysterious landscape of Arizona and Native American Art had a large impact on her. She lives in Tucson, where her favorite pastimes are creating art, enjoying her animals and exploring ghost towns.

DISCARD

Made in the USA
Columbia, SC
19 November 2018